Our Hero

THE
PURLOINING
OF
PRINCE
OLEOMARGARINE

. . . *Narrative should flow as flows the brook down through the hills and the leafy woodlands, its course changed by every boulder it comes across and by every grass-clad gravelly spur that projects into its path; its surface broken, but its course not stayed by rocks and gravel on the bottom in the shoal places; a brook that never goes straight for a minute, but goes, and goes briskly, sometimes ungrammatically, and sometimes fetching a horseshoe three-quarters of a mile around, and at the end of the circuit flowing within a yard of the path it traversed an hour before; but always going, and always following at least one law, always loyal to that law, the law of narrative, which has no law.*

—Mark Twain

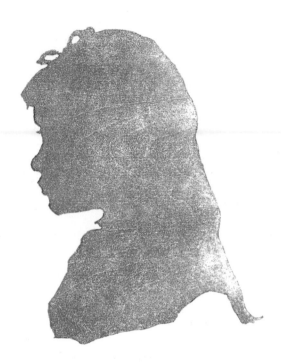

. . . I have wanted Papa to write a book that would reveal something of his kind sympathetic nature. . . .

—Susy Clemens

To the Clemens girls.
And our little girl, too.
—P.S. and E.S.

The publisher wishes to thank Dr. John Bird at Winthrop University, Dr. Robert Hirst at the Mark Twain Project and Papers at the University of California, Berkeley, Dr. Cindy Lovell, and the Mark Twain House & Museum in Hartford, Connecticut, for their generous and wise partnership in creating this book. Visit the Mark Twain House & Museum online at marktwainhouse.org and the Mark Twain Project and Papers at marktwainproject.org.

The original Mark Twain manuscript that inspired this book can be found online at PrinceOleomargarine.com.

THE
PURLOINING
OF
PRINCE
OLEOMARGARINE
— BY —
MARK TWAIN
— AND —
PHILIP STEAD
WITH ILLUSTRATIONS BY
ERIN STEAD

DOUBLEDAY BOOKS FOR YOUNG READERS

A NOTE FROM ONE OF THE AUTHORS

Hello,

My name is Philip Stead, which, if said too fast or too enthusiastically, sounds a lot like *Philip's dead!*—which I'm not. I am sure of it. Most likely, you don't know me and you've never heard my name, said too fast or otherwise. Chances are, though, you've heard of my friend Mr. Mark Twain. He's the one who told me this story, and, unlike me, he *is* dead. Or at least, I figure he is because three-quarter-ways into his delivery of the facts, he got up to fetch another cup of tea and vanished completely—*poof!*

I do hope he found that tea.

CHAPTER ONE

IN WHICH WE ARE INTRODUCED TO OUR LUCKLESS HERO

If we concentrate very carefully now, we will find ourselves in exactly the place we need to be. In fact, we will find ourselves in a land not all that far from here—not all that far, but hard enough to find that you're likely never to get there. I have tried. This land has a name, but it is much too difficult to pronounce. It would not be dignified to try.

Of course, *our* land, the United States of America, rolls effortlessly off the tongue and is so *easy* to find that you're likely to spend half your life looking for the way out. So already, you see, we've described two differences between Here and There.

Another difference to consider: In the hard-to-find-and-difficult-to-pronounce land in which our story takes place, the luckless and hungry remain luckless and hungry for all of their lives. By contrast, in the United States of America, everyone and everything is given a fair and equal chance. It would be rude to believe otherwise!

Here—be it Michigan or Missouri—the luckless and hungry are likely to stub a toe, look down, and discover at their feet a soup bowl full of gold bullion. *Eureka!* But *There,* the luckless and hungry are likely to stub a toe, look down, and discover only the dried-up root of a withered, old apple tree.

Which is exactly what Johnny, our hero, has just discovered—

"Eureka!" he exclaimed. He said *Eureka!*, and not something far worse, because long ago he'd made up his mind never to swear—not even when swearing was the necessity of a situation (as it often is). Johnny's poor, wretched grandfather swore often enough for the both of them. His cursings hung like a cloud over their unhappy home. Once, when Johnny was very young, a flock of pigeons became lost in this fog and dropped dead from despair, the whole lot of them belly-up on the roof. That is a fact. And it is, also, the reason that Johnny chose to carry a moral compass, in case he, too, ever became lost and needed to find his way.

Johnny had known no other family. And to say he knew his grandfather would be an optimism at best. And since a great many of the world's tragedies, big and small, were first thunk up in the minds of optimists, we will do humanity a favor now and stick to the cold facts:

Johnny's grandfather was a bad man.

Johnny's Grandfather

Johnny's only true companion was a melancholic chicken with a peculiar name. Her name was: *Pestilence and Famine*. Presumably at some time in the past, there were two chickens—one Pestilence and one Famine. But again, we must stick to the facts. Now there is one chicken, and she goes by two names.

Pestilence and Famine

Pestilence and Famine wandered over to peck weakly at Johnny's battered toe in sympathy.

"Thank you," said Johnny. "I think it will be alright." He hopped around on one foot. The chicken did likewise, thinking it the thing to do. Johnny smiled at his old friend.

This is how our chicken got her name—

For as long as Johnny could remember, his grandfather would greet the day by thundering out into the yard, kicking dirt into the air, and calling out to no one in particular, *Pestilence and famine! Pestilence and famine!* Pestilence and Famine thought this was great fun. She would set down her melancholy for a moment, prance around on skinny legs, and flap her ragged wings in delight. Then Johnny's grandfather would go inside, lie down on the dusty floor, and nap till well past noon. As he slept, he would coo softly and sing a gentle love song. This was when Johnny loved his grandfather best.

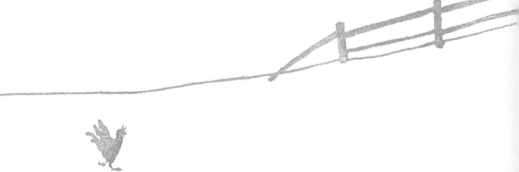

Johnny had never heard two words of kindness from his grand-father. And so it was a great surprise to Johnny when his grandfather stepped out of their broken-down shack and into the yard to ask, "Are you alright? Can you walk?"

Johnny's heart filled with happiness. "Yes!" he said. "I *will* be alright, thank you!"

"Good," replied his grandfather. "Then walk to market and sell that chicken for something worth eating."

CHAPTER TWO

REGARDING PARADES

Another difference between Here and There: roads.

In the United States of America, we have roads to everywhere. Ever since a boatful of bunglers first burgled this land from its Original Citizens, it has been our sacred duty to pave it all flat and crisscross every wilderness in rivers and streams of concrete. *Amen!*

In Johnny's land, there was only one road. People, and their chickens, seldom went anywhere. The road stretched in a straight, uwavering line with wildness, cruelty, and the threat of violence on either side for many uncharted miles and miles. At one forsaken end of this road was Johnny's humble home. At the other was the king's castle with its surrounding markets and squares and dancing and music, spontaneous outbursts of civic pride, mule racing, pickpocketing, robbery, vandalism, gambling, whippings, and everlasting parades. None of these things were known to Johnny, of course, as he had never left home in all of his life.

Johnny limped along with Pestilence and Famine trailing behind. The sun hung heavy in the sky overhead. Johnny stopped to mop his brow, allowing the miserable chicken time to catch up. "You will be better off," he said in a soft voice. Johnny hoped to offer some encouraging words to the dejected bird. "I have been your friend, but I can give you little else. With any luck, a kind farmer will take you in and feed you well." He reached down and patted Pestilence and Famine gently on the head. Johnny loved the chicken and had compassion for her troubles. He knew, though, what we all know—that the stories of too few chickens end happily. This is a fact and we must not ignore it.

The two friends pressed onward down the road in sorrowful single file. For three days they walked, chewing and pecking at tree bark when hunger rumbled in their bellies. They slept out in the open, and they slept very little. It was not a good time for anyone. But we will not dwell on the sad facts of this journey.

Instead we will save time and skip to the end.

They had just about reached their destination when suddenly, and without warning, Johnny and his chicken were swept up in a parade. There were trumpets and drums and far too many cymbals. There were flags and flaming batons, ridiculous uniforms and a multitude of silly hats. There was a man festooned in an excess of gold medallions, waving a saber wildly above his head (his reasons unclear). And there were throngs of joyous onlookers nearly fainting with delight. Of course, too, there was a cannon. (There is always a cannon.) Johnny did not see it, but he did hear it, and its deafening roar knocked him on his rear, nearly causing him to flatten his feathered friend and bring, prematurely, an end to her already less-than-dignified existence. Pestilence and Famine breathed a sigh and thought the thought of so many chickens before her: *Why me?*

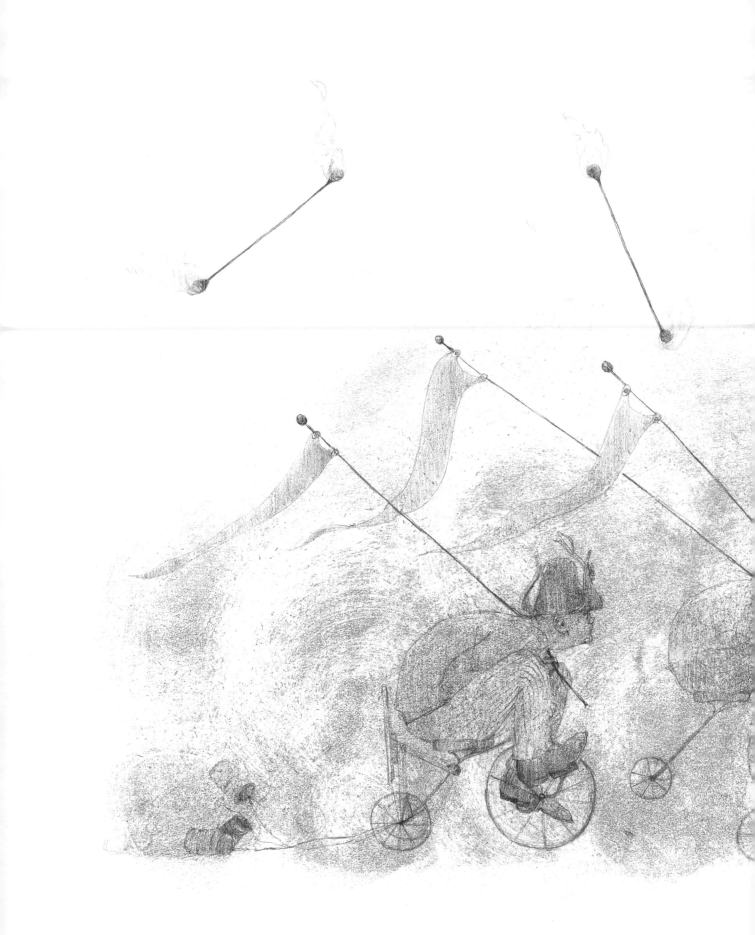

Parades are not for everyone. They are, rather, for people who like to wake up very, very early and make a lot of noise from the start. These qualities were not present in Johnny. Or in his chicken. So both now found themselves experiencing the kind of discomfort foreign to anyone accustomed to living life at enormous volumes.

Of course, it is my fondest wish to rescue Johnny from this repellent, predictable exercise and steal him away to a quiet place. But before doing so, I must mention that this *particular* parade had a strangeness worthy of note. All the paraders were hunched over as they marched, each one looking as if they'd dropped something very small and very important in the road. The cheering throngs were stooped over, too. In fact, the only ones anywhere standing fully at attention were the children. And the animals.

Johnny gathered his courage and asked a tired old donkey, "Excuse me, but why is everyone walking and standing in this way?"

The donkey brayed knowingly, but Johnny could not understand its meaning. A bearded man brandishing a hammer and possessing the unsavory look of optimism in his eyes spoke up in its place. "Step aside, lad!" He unfurled a scroll and fixed it to a tree near where Johnny stood. The tree groaned and accepted another spike in its rusty coat of nails. Johnny watched and wondered. If only the man would remove the many nails, maybe the tree would be released. Maybe it would walk along down the road into a better land. But for now, the tree was stuck. It wore the weight of many years' worth of forgotten proclamations, the newest of which read:

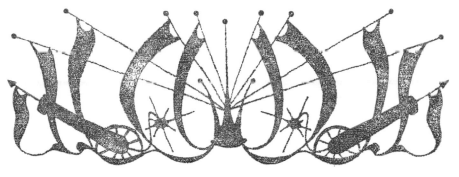

BY THE

KING

A PROCLAMATION

TODAY'S PARADE
IS TO CELEBRATE THE GLORIOUS VICTORIES
OF HIS MAJESTY'S ARMY
OVER THE MOST RECENT AND TERRIBLE
ENEMY TO THE NATION—
THE EXTREMELY TALL.
HIS HIGHNESS,
IN HIS INFINITE WISDOM AND PHYSICAL PROWESS,
HAS DEMONSTRATED THE APPROPRIATE MAXIMUM HEIGHT
FOR ALL MAN AND WOMANKIND.
HENCEFORTH
THOSE EXCEEDING HIS ELEVATION
ARE IN GROSS VIOLATION OF HIS AUTHORITY
AND ARE DEEMED, THEREFORE,
IN PERPETUITY
ENEMIES OF THE STATE.

Bearded Man

"Per-peh-tooooo-ih-tee," said the bearded man. He smiled the way certain men smile after winning something at someone else's expense.

Pestilence and Famine sat down in the road, weary of the excitement.

"Excuse me. Do you think—" started Johnny.

"We do not!" answered the man. And that was that. The band struck up a cacophony, and the whole company skedaddled down the road. Johnny and his woeful companion waited long enough to collect their discombobulation of nerves, then followed the cloud of dust left behind.

Not long from then, they found themselves in a bustling market in the great shadow of the castle wall.

ANOTHER NOTE FROM ONE OF THE AUTHORS

Because you did, I'm sure, take the time to read the author's note at the beginning of this book, you'll recall that this story is not my own. It was told to me by my friend Mr. Mark Twain.

Twain and I have a thing or two in common. For example, we both come from places beginning with the letter M. Me from Michigan and he from Missouri. There are many, many loathsome places to be from in this world, but none of them begin with the letter M. Not one!

Even still, Twain left Missouri and stayed for a while in Nevada, California, Hawaii, New York, London, Bombay, Pretoria, Florence, Paris, Egypt, Connecticut, and lots of other places not nearly as nice as the place he started out.

I have stayed in Michigan, mostly. So he came to me.

We met at a cabin on an island in the middle of Lake Michigan. The cabin smelled of freshly sawed wood. We sat outside in the sunshine on a cool September afternoon. He told this story (three-quarters of it, anyway) while I did what I do best, which is: look like I'm paying attention, but not. He drank tea, and I drank coffee. He talked, and I made notes of all the creatures that came to say hello:

A dragonfly.

A weasel.

Three black squirrels.

And, lastly, some kind of yellowish bird with black polka dots on its tail feathers. There are so many things to see in this world!

The island where we met has a name, which is: Beaver Island. A few hundred years ago, there were a lot of beavers on Beaver Island. But then some European travelers, balding and just passing through, realized those beavers looked a lot like fashionable hats. And *poof!*—no more beavers.

Another thing there used to be a lot of on Beaver Island is: friendly Mormon settlers. One hundred and seventy-some years ago, an optimist named James Jesse Strang led some nice folks to Beaver Island to start a colony. They built roads and bridges and lots of other useful things. They even had a newspaper. You know what its headline always read?

EVERYONE IS HAVING A GOOD TIME

James Jesse Strang declared himself king of the island, and everything was hunky-dory. That is, until King Strang made a few unpopular proclamations and ended up like pretty much all the beavers on Beaver Island—dead—with one important difference: No one made a hat out of Strang. Which was a kindness, I suppose.

Terrible things are always happening to kings. It makes you wonder why anyone would want the job at all. But that is no matter.

"What, then, became of the chicken?" I asked Mr. Twain.

CHAPTER THREE

THE RAREST OF BIRDS

Johnny walked through the market, unsure what strategy to take. There was noise and stink and careless violence all around. Johnny held Pestilence and Famine close to his chest to keep her from being trampled underfoot.

"Excuse me—" Johnny asked an ox. He paused, not certain what to say next. He was not practiced in the art of conversation.

But the ox was patient. He lay peacefully in the road, lost in a daydream.

Johnny could see the daydream in the ox's eyes. There were green fields and dandelions all around. But as Johnny stood there, clutching his sickly chicken and considering the dreams of an ox, there came a voice full of wild anger.

Ox in Daydream

"Back off!" it hollered. "The ox is mine!" Johnny turned and saw a man, bent sharply at the waist. He moved in a big, uncomfortable hurry, like everybody else. The man struck the animal with a long stick. "Move!" he shouted.

Johnny made way for the sad pair. But as he stepped backward, he stumbled—first on a bag of rabbit furs—then on an empty jug of whiskey—lastly into a turnip cart, which toppled over, spilling vegetables out into the road. The ox lowered his head and took a turnip in his teeth. This earned him another blow.

"Watch it, boy!" called the turnip man. He pushed Johnny into the road. Johnny fell, landing just shy of the wheels of a wagon clattering its way to the gallows. The prisoners hissed and spat at Johnny through their bars.

The day went along in this manner. And Johnny clung to the desperate bird throughout.

From time to time, Johnny looked up at the castle wall. In those moments, he realized the shabbiness of his own self—the holes in his clothes, the ragged scraps of leather strapped to his feet. He felt as though he carried on his back the weight of all the things he would never have. He tried to ignore his hunger. He tried to imagine himself an ox, standing in a field of tasty flowers. But he could not. So he sat down in the dirt and cried.

There came a gentle voice. "Alms for the poor?" it said.

Johnny looked up. Standing over him was an old, blind woman, thin enough to cast no shadow. She was very small. So small that even if she could unbend her bones and drop the weight of all her years, *still* she could stand up tall without fear of the king's wrath.

Despite her stature and her lowly condition, Johnny found the old woman beautiful. All her features were perfect—except for her left eye. Its color was wrong. Of course, this single hiccup in her biology only made her loveliness more astonishing and real.

"Alms for the poor?" she repeated. Hands shaking, she held out her wooden cup.

"I'm sorry," said Johnny. "I have nothing to give you. I have only this chicken. And if you could see her, you would know that that is *less* than nothing. She is irritable and unwell." He continued, "Still, you may have her if you can promise her a life even a little bit better than what she has known so far. She makes good company."

"I tell you this," Twain said to me, raising his teacup in the air, "there are more chickens than a man can know in this world, but an un-provoked kindness is the rarest of birds."

"Thank you," said the old woman. She put a hand on Johnny's shoulder and lowered herself to the ground. "Now I have something to give you." She reached inside her bag and pulled out a handful of pale blue seeds. She let them fall from her slender fingers into Johnny's palm. Each seed was the size of half a shirt button. Like the old woman, they were beautiful and plain. "These seeds," she explained, "were given to me, long ago, by an old woman to whom I had been kind. She was a fairy, I believe—"

"How did she know she was a fairy?" I asked.

"Because," answered Twain, "the woman in question was only four and a half inches tall. It was the scientific conclusion to make. Now, let's try not to interrupt, shall we?"

The old woman continued—

"Only in dire distress must the seeds be planted. Then, await the results with confidence. The seeds must be planted in spring, watered at dawn and exactly at midnight. Tend to them constantly, and keep a pure heart. Avoid complainings. When a flower comes up, eat it. It will make you full, and you will never feel emptiness again—"

Twain paused. A fly was swimming pitiful circles in his teacup.

"What happened next?" I asked.

"She died," said Twain.

"Right then?"

Twain rescued the fly with his spoon. "Would you rather she ate the chicken first?"

"No, I would *not* rather she ate the chicken first."

"Then perhaps write your own story—"

MY OWN STORY

The old woman gathered the chicken gently into her arms, stood up slowly, and walked away. As she walked, she sang a gentle love song—the words of which Johnny was surprised to know, and know well.

She did not die.

CHAPTER FOUR

WHAT HAPPENED NEXT

"Your version lacks credibility," said Twain. "Surely, the old woman is dead." He looked out over the lake. As he did, the fly landed in his cup a second time.

I said nothing.

"And it should be noted," he added, "that if Charles Darwin taught us anything, it is this: The chicken is dead, too. And lucky for her, because there are many unflattering ways to leave this world, but none quite so unflattering as being forced to live in it." He swallowed a mouthful of tea, then began to unfold the unpleasant events of Johnny's long journey home.

I wondered over the fate of the fly. Twain's relentless gloom had begun to bore me. So my mind began to drift.

It drifted as he described the barrenness of the land Johnny returned to, and the hunger that still gnawed at his innards.

It drifted as he described the whipping Johnny received when he presented his grandfather with a handful of pale blue seeds.

And it drifted as he described Johnny's grandfather, who took the seeds, chewed them up, and spat them on the ground. "Too bitter!" cried the old man. He kicked up a clod of earth and let fly a volley of obscenities.

"But every now and then," said Twain, "the gods take an unexpected holiday, and for a short time forget their obligation to add misery to the lives of the miserable. What other explanation can there be for what happened next?"

Johnny's grandfather lay down and died.

Johnny allowed himself a moment of perfect silence. Then he buried his grandfather, the only family he had ever known, under the empty branches of the apple tree. Johnny had no kind words to say. So, instead, he sang a gentle love song.

Then, because the gods were *still* out having a merry time, Johnny reached into his pocket and discovered, to his surprise, a single pale blue seed. He planted it there in the mound of dirt that covered the wicked old man.

Finally, one last bit of fortune came down from the heavens— it began to rain. It rained all day and all night. And though it was not enough rain to bring apples to the tree or grass from the ground, it was enough for Johnny to collect in cups and bowls and buckets.

It was the first day of spring.

Johnny watered his seed at dawn and exactly at midnight each day.

He tended his seed faithfully, pulling up weeds and scattering stones.

He kept a pure heart.

He avoided complainings.

And after a month's faithful watching, a green blade came up.

After a week, a bud appeared.

It blossomed full in another—a delicate pink flower with golden edging and a pale blue heart. Pretty and odd.

By now, Johnny's hunger was raging. He pulled the flower up from the roots and ate it. But the flower had no taste, and Johnny felt the emptiness in his belly even more than he had before.

Johnny's heart broke.

Tears flowed.

And he went sobbing into the wilderness to die—

CHAPTER FIVE

WHY THEY CALL IT BEAVER ISLAND

"Tell me again," said Twain, "why they call this Beaver Island?"

I reminded him about the hats.

"And I suppose no one consulted the beavers before uprooting them from their careful homes and placing them atop the heads of a few dozen Frenchmen?"

"No," I said, "I suppose not."

"And I suppose also," said Twain, "that no one thought to change the name of this place to something more suggestive of our new reality?"

I considered this. "There-Used-To-Be-Beavers Island is kind of a mouthful," I said.

"Clumsy, yes," said Twain, "but honest, no?"

CHAPTER SIX

WHAT HISTORY TELLS US

Johnny stretched out under an expanse of sky and waited for the end to come. He closed his eyes and thought of his old friend Pestilence and Famine. He wondered how she was getting along. He hoped she was happy and safe and well. As he lay there, he felt more alone than ever in his life.

"What is the matter?" asked a skunk.

Johnny opened his eyes with a start.

"Are you speaking?" asked Johnny. "To me?"

The skunk stood up on her hind legs and took a look around. "I believe so, yes."

There was a lengthy pause as Johnny experienced an untying of all the knots that had kept the riggings in his brain secure for so many years till now. "Could you repeat the question, please?" he asked.

"What is the matter?" asked the skunk a second time. "Are you okay?"

Johnny said nothing.

"Do you have a name?"

"Yes—Johnny," said Johnny.

"Fine, then," said the skunk. "My name is Susy. You look hungry. Follow me and we'll see that you are fed."

Susy

Twain sighed. "I know what you are thinking."

That my toes are cold? I thought.

"Sadly," he said, "there will *always* be those that turn up their noses at the sight of a skunk. But a boy who is friendless cannot afford to be concerned with the concerns of others. Nor should he! Because there is no greater friend than a skunk. They are decent, polite, and noble creatures. They deal honestly. They are slow to anger. And although capable of *spectacular* violence, the skunk walks with a gentle step."

I should have worn thicker socks, I thought.

"Of course," he added, "I could have saved myself—and Johnny—from the silly prejudices of the unenlightened. I could have lied and said *porcupine* or *kangaroo* instead of *skunk*.

"But if I lie to you once, you will never trust me again. And if history is our guide, our entire undertaking will be lost—

"Napoleon," he explained, "lied to his men at Waterloo. He said: *We are going to have a great time!* They did not.

"King Henry VIII lied to Anne Boleyn, and the whole thing caused nothing but headaches.

"There are other examples, too!—

"Consider George Washington. He made an awful stink about the nobleness of truth telling *after* the fact, but the sad reality is this—he looked that cherry tree dead in the face and told it: *This won't hurt a bit*.

"History tells us these things. And we can trust history on the matter of lies because history is *mostly* lies, along with some exaggerations."

"Are your feet getting cold?" I asked.

Twain ignored me. He added two spoonfuls of sugar to his teacup and continued—

As you know, there was only one road in Johnny's kingdom. There were, however, many pathways known only to the animals. It was along one of these pathways that Johnny followed his new companion, over hills and through valleys and canyons with the sheer faces of cliffs rising on either side. When they came to a stream, Susy hopped from stone to stone to keep from getting wet. Johnny took a drink, then waded straight through to cool his aching feet. At the entrance to a wild orchard, blooming full and fragrant, Johnny looked around and realized he was, in fact, so completely lost that he had no choice but to follow the skunk deeper still into the wildness of unknown country.

"Do you need a rest?" asked Susy.

"No, thank you," said Johnny. He followed along, walking slowly, as is the way with skunks—they are never in a hurry. "Excuse me," he asked. "How is it that you can talk?"

"All animals can talk," Susy replied. She stopped to brush away a fly with a whip of her tail. "We often speak to humans, but get no reply we can understand. The talk of humans is incomprehensible and, I suspect, dull."

Then she explained, "A lion can speak to a squirrel can speak to an owl can speak to a mouse. A camel can speak to a pig can speak to an elk can speak to an elephant. A whale can speak to a gull. A giraffe can speak to a hermit crab. It is only humans that no one can understand. It is why they are so ignorant and backward and lonely and sad—they have so few creatures to talk to." Susy added, "But I do not mean to offend. You do not seem ignorant or backward."

"But you understand *me*?" asked Johnny.

"Yes," answered Susy, "for evidently you have eaten the juju flower. It is rarely given to anybody."

Johnny and Susy passed through the end of the orchard. On the other side was an open meadow of tall grasses and wildflowers, one hundred yards wide and one hundred yards long. They walked to the center, and Susy called to a yellow finch perched on a blade of tall grass. Susy spoke something too quiet for Johnny to hear, and the finch flew off in a blink.

"It will only be a moment now," said Susy.

Minutes later, they were surrounded by all the animals in the land (almost all the animals, that is, for the tiger was missing). The news had flown to every corner. Clouds and droves of joyous birds and beasts collected to see the boy who had eaten the juju flower.

Johnny was overwhelmed by the sight.

"Make a speech!" called the jackrabbit.

Johnny opened his mouth but could not find the words. The bottom had dropped completely out of his vocabulary.

"It is okay to be shy," said Susy quietly, so as not to embarrass him. "Even just a few words will suffice."

Johnny took a deep breath to calm his nerves. Then he opened his mouth and discovered the words that could save mankind from all its troubles, if only mankind could say them once in a while and make them truly meant. He said:

"I am glad to be here."

And a cheer went up.

CHAPTER SEVEN

THE BANQUET

Preparations were made to welcome Johnny and to make him feel comfortable. The moles dug a cellar and stocked it full. The beavers (because there were still more than a few left in this land) erected posts and covered them with boughs and branches. Great tangles of vines were dragged in by the deer, and the raccoons wove them together into sheets to make walls. Earth was placed on top, and tall flowers planted there, giving the beginnings of Johnny's unlikely home the look of having sprouted right up from the ground. The mice chewed two small doorways for themselves, one for coming and one for going. Johnny took up his saw and did the same—

The Moles

"Where did he get the saw?" I asked.

Twain sighed and shook his head. I do not think he could bear sometimes to hear other people talk. "Our boy," he answered, "has the entire animal kingdom at his disposal. Do you not think he could trouble a few of its feathered members to fly off and steal a saw?"

"Maybe," I answered. "But I'd say your version lacks credibility."

"And yet," said Twain, "here we are just the same—"

Lastly, Johnny cut two windows, one on either side of the front door. One was just the right height for Johnny to look out and marvel at all the life that surrounded him. The other was just the right height for curious animals of a certain size to look in and wonder at the unusual creature that was now in their company.

"Does he always walk on two legs?" wondered a salamander.

"Does he swim?" wondered a muskrat.

"How long will he stay?" wondered a squirrel. "And what does he eat?"

But before these questions could be answered, Susy peered inside and announced, "The party is about to begin!"

A banquet was prepared. Cherries and nuts and strawberries, and every other good thing that could be found, were brought together and piled high. The cow was milked. Bread was baked. The tiger—who had been missing from the proceedings so far—arrived now at the smell of dinner. Ample space was made for her.

When everyone was gathered together, Susy raised her tail, causing a hush to fall over the assembly. She said, "How exciting that today we have found a new friend! Now let's eat and all have a good time—"

Johnny took the first bite—a warm, crusty slice of bread covered over with butter and smashed raspberries. He had never tasted anything so good. Johnny ate till he was full, and the animals ate till *they* were full, and all were happy and satisfied—except, of course, for the tiger, who cared little for nuts and berries and milks and breads. She had a different kind of tooth.

When dinner was nearly done, the nightingale excused herself.
She shook the crumbs from her feathers and flew up to a high branch.
From there, she sang a sweet song. It had no words, but still, everyone
present knew its meaning, which was:

The world is beautiful and dangerous,

and joyful and sad,

and ungrateful and giving,

and full of so, so many things.

The world is new and it is old.

It is big and it is small.

The world is fierce and it is kind,

and we, every one of us,

are in it.

"Thank you," said the nightingale. "Good night." She flew off to find her nest, and in her place rose the monkey, who made this speech:

Or, rather, he *would've* made a speech, except the whole thing was lost because Twain was near to drowning himself in laughter from the first word on. The monkey sure could deliver a joke.

Next came the lion.

He stood up and spoke powerfully in a sober tone:

"Today, as we meet to celebrate a new brother in our fold, we must remember all the brothers and sisters we have lost. Every time of gladness reminds us of a time of grief. And until we find a way to live in perfect peace, we must mourn for those we have known and loved and surrendered to the natural laws that govern us all."

The tiger, watching now from a dark spot between the trees, turned up her lip in a menacing grin. She stayed quiet, though, keeping the mutterings of her stomach to herself.

The Lion

The banquet was ended.

Susy walked with Johnny to the door of his new home. The animals followed, nestling in around Johnny's home and retiring to their branches and holes and hollows. The buzzard brought Johnny the hide of a seal, washed and picked clean. Johnny lay down and wrapped himself up in it.

That night, he slept more soundly and more peacefully than ever in his life—surrounded by so many friends.

The tiger stayed up awhile, heading into the dark to hunt.

CHAPTER EIGHT

PRINCE OLEOMARGARINE
IS MISSING!

The lark called all hands at daylight. One by one, the animals awoke and began their morning routines. Johnny, having no routine in this new life, stood in his doorway, amazed by all the activity at such an early hour. He scratched his head and wondered what *he* ought to be doing.

Susy recognized Johnny's worry. "This way," she said, and she led him down a narrow path through a cluster of young trees. They had taken only a few steps before the bustle and noise of the morning was far behind them. A few steps more and they were standing at the bank of a clear blue pond. "Here is a good place to wash and have a drink," said the skunk. Then she settled into a circle of moss and waited for him. When he was clean, she took him to a cluster of huckleberry bushes nearby. There, they sat and had a quiet breakfast.

That day, and each day following, Johnny and the animals wandered over mountains and through forests, picnicking and frolicking and taking long naps in the sun. Everyone was having a good time. At the end of each day, Johnny returned to his home at the edge of the wild orchard.

For the first time in Johnny's life, everything was going well—

"And," said Twain, "since there is nothing more boring than a barrage of good cheer, we will stop the story here and skip ahead to a suggestion of future peril—"

They came upon a handbill nailed to the trunk of an old oak tree, its ink still wet.

"What does it say?" asked Susy.

All the animals huddled in close as Johnny read aloud:

REWARD

PRINCE OLEOMARGARINE
IS MISSING!

GIANTS SUSPECTED

HIS MAJESTY, THE KING,
BEGS HIS DUTIFUL SERVANTS
TO STEP FORWARD WITH INFORMATION
LEADING TO THE SAFE RETURN
OF THE NATION'S OWN SON.
MONEY, A PRINCESS,
AND A HOME IN THE PALACE FOR LIFE
AWAIT THE BRAVE SOUL WHO ANSWERS
HIS MAJESTY'S DESPERATE PLEA.

"Well?" asked Susy. "Would you like to earn that money?"

Johnny thought for a moment. He had never *had* money before. It sounded like a very nice thing to have. "Yes," he answered. "I think so."

"Alright," said Susy, "then go and tell the king exactly this: *If you protect my witnesses, I'll give you news of the prince.* Say nothing more."

CHAPTER NINE

WHAT SUSY KNEW

Of course, Susy knew that Johnny did not need money. Or a princess. Or even a home in the palace for life. But perhaps also she knew this: If she guided Johnny to the edge of the animals' world, and if she stood him up on a mountaintop looking down at the castle below, Johnny would have the courage and the bravery to continue on his own. The castle guards might greet him with laughter. They might scour him with ridicule and howl with glee at his request: "I am here to see the king." But as long as Johnny felt the watchful eyes of his friends from far above, he could bear any insult with the quiet confidence of a skunk.

"I come with news of the prince," he said calmly.

And with that, the two guards whisked Johnny through the gate and into the castle, stumbling and bungling and begging his pardon all the way.

The Castle Guards

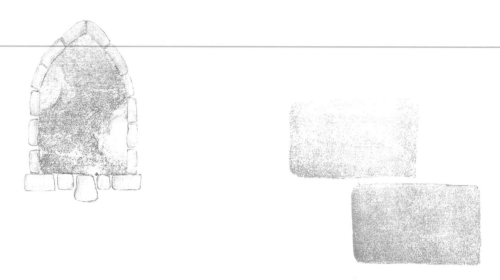

They led the boy up winding flights of stairs, past rooms of blue silk, and rooms of red silk, and rooms done up in shining, glowing colors that Johnny had never seen before.

They led him through marbled halls with ceilings clad in gold.

They led him down long corridors lined with tapestries that told the stories of kingdoms won and lost and forgotten.

Johnny marveled at these wonders, and as he did, the guards led him through a colossal door, twenty feet high and ten feet wide, made from long bands of carved ivory. The carvings told stories, bloody and mean. On the other side of the terrible door was the royal throne, where His Highness was sitting, having himself a snooze.

His Highness

The royal guards stepped forward and roused the king.

"What, what is it?!" shouted His Highness.

"Beg pardon, Your Majesty, but the boy, he says he has news of the prince."

"Yes?! Yes?!" said the king. He struggled up out of his chair, weighed down by a ridiculous hodgepodge of ill-fitting robes and heavy jewels. Beside him sat the queen—peacefully, carefully working at her knitting.

The king's crown slipped down over his eyes. "Where is this boy?" he hollered. "Show yourself! Speak!"

"Your Majesty?" spoke Johnny.

The king's countenance sank as he lifted his crown and laid eyes on the unlikely messenger. "And what *exactly*," he asked, "can someone as insignificant as *you* do for my trouble?"

The king's words wounded Johnny. But the hardships of life had developed in him a power to conceal all but the biggest hurts. He delivered Susy's message coolly, and without emotion: "If you protect my witnesses, King, I'll give you news of the prince."

The king was indignant. "Who are these witnesses?" he demanded. "Let the cowards step forward! Let them tell of the purloining of Prince Oleomargarine!"

"Your Majesty?" begged Johnny. He did not understand. "The purr-who?"

"The pur*loining,* boy!" answered the king.

Johnny said nothing.

His Majesty spoke more loudly and more slowly now, so as not to confound the poor boy's wits. "PURRRRR-LOYYYYY-NINNNG!" he bellowed.

"TAKE NOTE!" boomed Twain, his voice carrying out over the enormous lake. "Never place your trust in a man overly impressed with his own vocal cords. Honest men—and women—speak plainly, and at normal volumes."

"Stolen," explained the queen. She looked up from her knitting and spoke directly to Johnny in a soft voice. Few had ever spoken to him in this way. He thought back to the old, blind woman. "The prince has been stolen—"

"—by giants!" finished the king. "Loathsome, terrible giants! Scourge of the nation!"

"Of course," said the queen, "we are not *entirely* sure he was stolen at all."

The king ignored his wife, as was his custom.

Twain took one last sip of tea and set down an empty cup. "There are men who cannot hear animals," he said. "And then there are men who cannot hear anything at all."

The Queen

The busy clatter of the queen's knitting needles filled the cavernous throne room.

Unsure what to say, Johnny remained quiet.

"Very well," said the king. "I'll promise anything. I'll line the streets with soldiers, and none shall touch your witnesses—*whoever* they may be."

"Thank—" started Johnny. But the king interrupted, delivering instead this speech to all those unlucky enough to be in attendance:

"MY . . . FAITHFUL . . . SON," he began, full of grandiloquent bombast, "is the joy of this nation! He is as clever as a fox, and as strong as an elephant! He is magnificent in battle, and handsomer than every boy his age! He has immaculate teeth! He is an excellent speller! And someday he will grow up to slay one hundred thousand giants!" The king exhaled loudly, finishing, "He is like *Me* in every way. That is to say—perfect. He *must* be returned."

The royal napkin was produced to wipe a single tear from the king's cheek.

"Now," said His Majesty, "you may go."

"Thank you," said Johnny.

And he left to gather his friends—

"These? *These* are your witnesses?" implored the king.

The lion gave a mighty roar, rattling the bones of the entire assembly.

"He tells me they are ready to testify," said Johnny.

"Who?" asked the king. "Who tells you?"

Johnny answered, "The lion, Your Highness."

There followed now a moment of bumfuzzlement inside the hollow sitting room of the little king's noggin. "I cannot believe it," he said. "Give me proof." He rose and pointed to the back of the room. "Speak to that bird over there, the unattractive one with the disagreeable look on its face. Tell it to place a feather in my royal guard's cap."

Johnny translated this message for the buzzard.

The bird took flight, landing on the guard's shoulder and plucking a long yellow hair from inside his ear.

"Marvelous!" cried the king. "If he weren't but a poor, dumb bird, he just might've got it! Now order your lion to chase its tail."

Johnny translated this message for the lion.

The lion growled, and everyone present felt the air quiver and shake.

"He refuses your request," said Johnny. "It is beneath his station."

The king was convinced. "Let the evidence proceed!"

CHAPTER TEN

THE WITNESSES TESTIFY

The tiger began—

"I lay in my lair and saw two strong men pass by with the prince."

"As I suspected," exclaimed the king, "giants!"

The queen sighed and shook her head.

"I could not manage the precipice," continued the tiger, "so I notified the eagle overhead. He followed them."

Said the eagle—

"I followed them till dark, then notified the owl."

Said the owl—

"I followed them till I came to the sea, then notified the gull."

Said the gull—

"I followed them across the waters, then tired as they entered the reedy marsh. I asked for the alligator."

Said the alligator—

"I followed them to the hot edge of the desert, then notified the sand snake."

Said the snake—

"I followed them to the grassy plain, then notified the antelope."

Said the antelope—

"I followed them to the snowy highlands, then notified the reindeer."

Said the reindeer—

"I followed them up the summit, then notified the mouse."

Said the mouse—

"I slipped past two mighty dragons that guarded the mouth of a dark cave, then called for the bat."

Said the bat—

"I followed them in. I know the place. The prince is there still."

The king was aghast. "Go now!" he ordered. "Find my son and bring him back! You shall have your reward!"

The queen had finished her knitting. "Wait," she said. "Before you go, child, come here."

Johnny stepped forward.

The queen placed a red scarf around Johnny's neck and kissed him softly. "Good luck," she said. Then the king's wife stood up and, towering a full foot and a half above the head of her husband, bid them all goodbye.

Johnny and the animals bowed and departed.

As he left, the elephant tore the ivory door from its hinges.

ONE FINAL NOTE FROM ONE OF THE AUTHORS

It was around about now that Mr. Twain got up to fetch another cup of tea and made like pretty much all the beavers on Beaver Island—*poof!*

Which really left me hanging.

I finished my coffee, alone. As I did, I sat there daydreaming and wondering about Johnny and Susy and all the rest. I looked beside me and considered the empty space my friend had left behind. I allowed myself a moment of perfect silence. The last sliver of sun sank below the lake, painting the sky in a wash of brilliant colors. *There are so many things to see in this world!* It was then I noticed it, right there on the arm of Twain's chair—a pink flower with golden edging and a pale blue heart. Pretty and odd.

I don't know why I ate the flower, but I did. I wasn't even hungry! I thought, *It's amazing, the things that people do sometimes.*

"Excuse me," came a voice. A small voice, near my feet.

I looked down, and standing there staring back at me was a weasel—possibly the same one as before (they are very tricky to tell apart). *This is an interesting turn of events,* I thought.

"Are you just going to eat and eat and offer me nothing?" he said.

I went inside and came back with a cracker.

The weasel held the cracker with both paws, and began nibbling in a careful spiral. "It is so refreshing to be understood," he said, his cheeks full.

I poured myself another cup of coffee. "Would you like to hear a story?" I asked.

"I suppose," said the weasel, "if you have more snacks."

I went inside, bringing back a peanut butter cookie and half a carrot. The weasel got to work. I sat back down and began the story with:

If we concentrate very carefully now, we will find ourselves in exactly the place we need to be. In fact, we will find ourselves in a land not all that—

"Does this place have a name?" Interrupted the weasel. "I haven't got all day."

"It does," I said. But I couldn't remember what it was. So I lied. "It is called There-Used-To-Be-Beavers Island."

From there, I continued on, delivering Twain's story pretty much just like I heard it, right up till the part where—*poof!*—Twain disappeared and I found myself chatting with an impatient but amiable ball of fur.

"Could we hurry this up?" asked the weasel. "I don't mean to be rude, but it's getting late. And I have a busy night ahead."

I looked and saw that the moon had arrived above the darkening lake.

"Maybe just skip to the end?" he suggested.

"The end?" Twain had not supplied me with an ending.

"You *do* have an ending," said the weasel. He picked a crumb of cookie from the white fur on his chest and popped it in his mouth. "The ending is, after all, the only part that really matters."

I swallowed the remainder of my coffee, buying myself a moment to think.

CHAPTER ELEVEN

THE ONLY PART THAT REALLY MATTERS

They stood at the entrance to a great cave flanked on either side by two ornery dragons. The dragons did not at first notice Johnny or the many animals gathered around him. They were otherwise occupied—

"Blue!" shouted dragon number one.

"No! Red!" spat dragon number two.

An important thing to know about dragons is this: They are always arguing with one another. No two dragons can agree on anything.

"Yellow!" cried one.

"Green!" cried the other.

The correct answer was, in fact: purple. But neither would admit it. They would sooner set the entire forest ablaze. The two dragons bickered back and forth, spitting fire and singeing the luckless shrubberies nearby with their careless anger.

"Excuse me?" asked Johnny.

Startled, the dragons swung around to confront the unexpected stranger. Smoke poured from their nostrils. They each took a step forward, eager to make trouble—

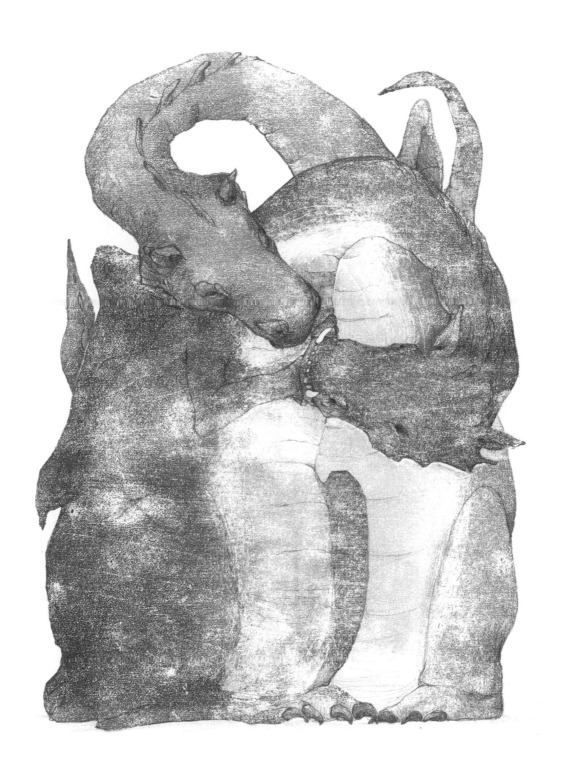

Two Ornery Dragons

"Exciting!" said the weasel. He had climbed up onto Twain's chair, pulling his chin to the table's edge to look for crumbs.

"You might think so, yes," I answered. "And you might think, also, that a story can be properly told in the face of constant interruption. But, sadly, you are wrong. Because this story is a mess. And even though you may expect Johnny to lead his troops fearlessly into battle—"

"I do!"

"And even though you may expect Johnny, who is facing spectacular odds, to emerge victorious and none the worse for wear—"

"He will!"

"And even though you may expect Johnny to carry with him for the rest of his life the lessons supposedly learned in war—"

"Always bring a snack!"

"He will not. Because the lessons of war are too heavy to carry. And besides, at that very moment Susy climbed out from inside Johnny's shirt—where she'd been enjoying a luxurious afternoon nap—and the dragons did next what a great many mighty creatures do when suddenly and unexpectedly encountering a skunk, which is: panic and flee—"

"This way!" cried dragon number one.

"No, that way!" cried dragon number two.

Terrified, they flew off in opposite directions.

"Did I miss anything?" asked Susy.

"I don't think so, no," said Johnny. Then he, Susy, Pestilence and Famine, and all the other animals entered the cave undisturbed.

The tiger, who'd been watching from a comfortable distance, slunk in behind—

———

"The chicken is back?" asked the weasel.

"Yes," I answered, "the chicken is back."

The weasel frowned. Twain had left him no crumbs.

"It is not my fault," I explained, "that you chose to skip to the end of the story, and therefore robbed yourself of the surprising and uplifting events that have unfolded in the life of this particular chicken—"

"Whose fault is it?" asked the weasel.

"Of course, there is no logical reason why Johnny would reunite with his bird. It makes no sense. But logic and fact are two different things—and the fact of the matter is this: It is my story now and the chicken is back."

"But whose fault is it?" asked the weasel.

"I don't know," I sighed, continuing—

———

The cave was dark. Very dark. Johnny felt as though he had been swallowed up into the belly of a dragon. *I am afraid*, he thought. But then he heard the quiet footsteps of all the animals behind him. He felt the soft fur of Susy's tail brush against his ankle. And he decided to be brave. He remembered how an old friend used to make light in a bad situation, and he decided to do the same: Johnny hopped up and down on one leg. Pestilence and Famine did likewise, thinking it the thing to do.

As Johnny was discovering his courage, his eyes began to make sense of the dark. Slowly, slowly, a sea of troubled faces came into focus.

"Are you the giants?" asked Johnny.

"We are taller than the king, yes," said one.

"And we prefer not to slouch," added another.

"Hideous, villainous ogres!" called a voice. The voice had all the qualities of a tin can nailed to the hoof of a horse. Prince Oleomargarine burst forth.

"Have you come for the prince?" asked the giants wearily. They addressed the skunk now. (It is not wise to take your eyes off a skunk.)

"We have," answered Susy—but they did not understand.

Johnny translated for the giants. "We have," he said.

"Please, then, take him," they pleaded. "He attacked us in the road. And although we begged him to leave, he followed us back to this cave— the one safe place we have known since war was declared and our troubles began. He has terrible manners and a foul mouth. He eats everything in sight—"

Now, it should be noted that if Charles Darwin taught us anything, it is this: There are many accidents of biology that are beyond our control. Some of us are short, some of us are tall. Some of us are weak, some of us are strong. Thankfully, though, personalities are not born ugly; they are learned ugly. Our prince may have been a perfect reflection of his father, but it could've been the other way. He could've been kind. Sadly, the prince spoke up now, assuring us all that hope for him was lost—

"Filthy giants!" he hollered. "Abominations!" Then he spelled it: "A-B-O-M-I-N-A-S-H-U-N-S!" The prince turned to Johnny, eyeing him with disgust. "And I demand a better rescuer!" he declared. His Royal Highness, joy of the nation, sat down on the cave floor and began to pout.

The tiger stepped forward without a sound. "*I* will take the boy," she offered in a low, silky purr. She continued, speaking directly to the prince, "You may ride on my back. You are a handsome boy and are just the right size. When you are hungry, I will hunt for you, and you can eat all that I kill. I will be your servant and your pet. Someday, when you are king, you can take my hide and lay it on the floor of your throne room."

Johnny translated for His Excellency.

"I have immaculate teeth," announced Oleomargarine for no reason whatsoever, adding, "Will we kill giants?"

The tiger answered, "We will do *only* what comes naturally to us." She licked her chops and waited for His Majesty's reply.

Prince Oleomargarine was persuaded. "Alright! Let's go!" He mounted the tiger and exited the cave—leaving our story and entering another with an ending far more satisfying than this.

Prince Oleomargarine

"What now?" asked the giants. "Will you reveal our secret place?"

"No, we will not," answered Susy.

"No, we will not," translated Johnny.

"Do you not hate us?" asked the giants.

Johnny did not need to translate the skunk's reply. Her answer was understood from the kindness in her eyes.

The giants turned to Johnny. "And you?" they asked. "Do *you* hate us?"

Johnny opened his mouth but could not find the words. Once again, the bottom had dropped completely out of his vocabulary.

"It's okay," said the skunk. "Just tell the truth."

But before we find an answer for Johnny, let us describe one more difference between Here and There—

Here, a young boy of Johnny's age can collect piles and piles of money, and with that money he can buy all the things he will ever need. But *There*—in Johnny's land—all the money you can ever find will not afford you even *one* of the most important things around, which is: A true friend.

Johnny looked up and was overwhelmed by all his riches.

"Go ahead," whispered Susy.

Johnny took a deep breath to calm his nerves. Then he opened his mouth and discovered the words that could save mankind from all its silly, ceaseless violence, if only mankind could say them once in a while and make them truly meant. He said:

"I am glad to know you."

And the giants wept.

THE END

"Bravo!" cried the weasel. "Do you have another cookie?"

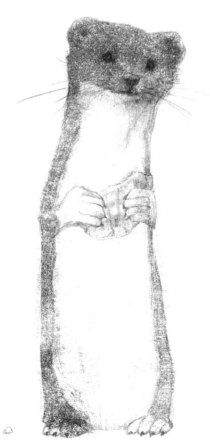

EPILOGUE

WHAT BECAME OF THE CHICKEN

She lived to be one hundred years old.

———

"Chickens do not live that long," said the weasel.

———

This one did.

A NOTE FROM THE EDITOR

When your father is Mark Twain, it is not too much to expect a well-told bedtime story every night. Twain's young daughters Clara and Susy knew as much, and in an 1879 journal entry Twain writes about just such a domestic moment in a Paris hotel:

> [W]hen my day's writing, on the 6th floor, was done, I used to slip quietly into our parlor on the 2nd floor, hoping to have a rest and a smoke on the sofa before dinner was brought up; but I seldom succeeded, because the nursery opened into the parlor and the children were pretty sure to come in for something and discover me—then I would have to take a big chair, place a child on each arm of it, and spin them a story.

The nightly ritual went as such: Clara would choose a magazine, flip to a picture as a story prompt, and say, "We're ready, Papa."

As Twain recalls, "Their selections were pretty odd." He describes how one evening, thumbing through *Scribner's,* the girls chose an anatomical figure drawing. His attempts to divert them to a more romantic image spurned, Twain gave in ("I bent myself to the task") and began the tale of a boy named Johnny. The story was "such a thrilling and rattling success" that Twain was "rewarded with the privilege of digging a brand-new story out of that barren text during the next *five ensuing evenings.*"

Sometime later, Twain committed notes from this storytelling session to paper. Jotted down in disconnected bursts, they begin: "Widow, dying, gives seeds to Johnny—got them from old woman once, to whom she had been kind." They end abruptly sixteen pages later with a cliff-hanger: "It is guarded by 2 mighty dragons who never sleep." The tale was never written and the story left unfinished. Although Twain told his daughters countless fairy tales, the notes for this particular week of stories are believed to be the only ones he ever wrote down.

After Twain's death, the notes went to the Mark Twain Papers archive at the University of California, Berkeley. In 2011, Dr. John Bird, a Twain scholar at Winthrop University, noticed the story fragment in the Berkeley archive while searching for food-related material for a possible Twain cookbook. He had asked to look at the file because it contained the word "Oleomargarine." It was then that he identified the story as an unfinished children's fairy tale, one that matched up with Twain's journal entry about his storytelling session in Paris. Dr. Robert Hirst, General Editor of the Mark Twain Papers, believes this was the first time anyone had scrutinized these notes and recognized their importance.

Dr. Bird shared them with Dr. Cindy Lovell, then Executive Director of the Mark Twain House & Museum in Hartford, Connecticut. And in 2014, Doubleday Books for Young Readers acquired the rights to work with the Mark Twain House & Museum and the Mark Twain Papers to create a brand-new work, using Twain's notes as its foundation.

But where does one turn with a set of rough notes for a fragmentary and unfinished story told well over a hundred years ago? If fortune is on one's side, one turns to Philip and Erin Stead, the Caldecott Medal–winning author and illustrator of *A Sick Day for Amos McGee*. Philip used Twain's notes as the starting point for the book you hold now, imagining it as a tale buttressed by conversations between Philip and Twain himself. Retreating to Beaver Island in Lake Michigan, Philip began with Twain's story arc and specific quotes from Twain's notes, then wove a 10,000-

word manuscript that seamlessly blended his own work with Twain's. Erin Stead, using techniques both old and new—wood carving, ink, pencil, and a laser cutter—created the sly, humorous, and touchingly beautiful illustrations that illuminate this new work.

It is, quite literally, a book that reaches through time. The story of Johnny, conceived from an anatomical figure in a nineteenth-century magazine, is now a tale for today's Twain fans, young and old. It is a story of goodness, honor, and courage in the face of tyranny, told with a humor and inventiveness we hope Mark Twain—and Clara and Susy—would have endorsed.

The Mark Twain House

word manuscript that seamlessly blended his own work with Twain's. Erin Stead, using techniques both old and new—wood carving, ink, pencil, and a laser cutter—created the sly, humorous, and touchingly beautiful illustrations that illuminate this new work.

It is, quite literally, a book that reaches through time. The story of Johnny, conceived from an anatomical figure in a nineteenth-century magazine, is now a tale for today's Twain fans, young and old. It is a story of goodness, honor, and courage in the face of tyranny, told with a humor and inventiveness we hope Mark Twain—and Clara and Susy—would have endorsed.

session to paper. Jotted down in disconnected bursts, they begin: "Widow, dying, gives seeds to Johnny—got them from old woman once, to whom she had been kind." They end abruptly sixteen pages later with a cliff-hanger: "It is guarded by 2 mighty dragons who never sleep." The tale was never written and the story left unfinished. Although Twain told his daughters countless fairy tales, the notes for this particular week of stories are believed to be the only ones he ever wrote down.

After Twain's death, the notes went to the Mark Twain Papers archive at the University of California, Berkeley. In 2011, Dr. John Bird, a Twain scholar at Winthrop University, noticed the story fragment in the Berkeley archive while searching for food-related material for a possible Twain cookbook. He had asked to look at the file because it contained the word "Oleomargarine." It was then that he identified the story as an unfinished children's fairy tale, one that matched up with Twain's journal entry about his storytelling session in Paris. Dr. Robert Hirst, General Editor of the Mark Twain Papers, believes this was the first time anyone had scrutinized these notes and recognized their importance.

Dr. Bird shared them with Dr. Cindy Lovell, then Executive Director of the Mark Twain House & Museum in Hartford, Connecticut. And in 2014, Doubleday Books for Young Readers acquired the rights to work with the Mark Twain House & Museum and the Mark Twain Papers to create a brand-new work, using Twain's notes as its foundation. But where does one turn with a set of rough notes for a fragmentary and unfinished story told well over a hundred years ago? If fortune is on one's side, one turns to Philip and Erin Stead, the Caldecott Medal–winning author and illustrator of A Sick Day for Amos McGee. Philip used Twain's notes as the starting point for the book you hold now, imagining it as a tale buttressed by conversations between Philip and Twain himself. Retreating to Beaver Island in Lake Michigan, Philip began with Twain's story arc and specific quotes from Twain's notes, then wove a 10,000-